*To the
Peninsula Humane Society
with thanks for
our Lobo*

Lothrop, Lee & Shepard Co. ❧ New York

LOBO

by Gladys Yessayan Cretan

illustrated by
Patricia Coombs

Lobo was the littlest dog in the neighborhood.

He was black.
He could run like the wind.

He was brave.

But everyone talked about how small he was.
"He's no bigger than a minute," they said.

Lobo looked over his shoulder.
"I'm not little," he thought. "I go all the way
to the tip of my tail."

When Lobo's family moved to a new house the
neighbors asked about his name.

"It means wolf," Peter said.

"He doesn't look like a wolf," said the neighbors.

"He's such a little dog."

"I'm not little," Lobo thought.

He ran across the yard and barked at a caterpillar.
"I'm fierce."

He sat in the front hall, near the door.
"I'm guarding the family," he said to himself.
"I'm loyal."

When he heard footsteps he cocked his head.

It was a stranger!

He barked. He growled and he barked again.

The family came running.

"Oh, Lobo," Mary Ann said. "It's the new milkman."

Lobo stopped to think. Peter liked milk.
Perhaps the milkman should be allowed.

Peter's mother opened the door.
"My," said the milkman. "Such a small dog
making all that noise."

"I'm not small," thought Lobo.
He ran outside and chased all the birds off the
back lawn.
"The birds know I'm big," he said to himself.

All afternoon Lobo was busy.

"I'm a watchdog. I must do my duty."

He barked at the laundryman, the telephone man.

"Stop! Stop!" called Peter.

"You can't be too careful," Lobo thought.
He barked at the newspaper boy, at the neighbors.

"Quiet!" yelled Mary Ann.
Lobo barked on.

"Shame on you, Lobo," said Mrs. McGee. "All that noise."

"You're a bad dog," Mary Ann said.

"You're only a little dog," Peter said, "so start acting like one."

Lobo walked off slowly.

He found a bush to hide under. He put his head
down on his paws.

"I'm not little," he said to himself. "Am I?"
No one answered.

When Peter came out and called him, Lobo stayed right where he was, under the bush.

"He knows he's in disgrace," Mary Ann said. "Don't worry, he'll come out later."

"No," thought Lobo. "I won't come out all day and all night. And they'll be sorry." Though he wasn't sure why.

He tried not to think about the good food in his red dish. He tried not to think about the secret treats Peter slipped to him under the dining room table. He tried not to notice when Peter and Mary Ann went to play with their new friends next door.

But he was lonely.

Little by little, sleep sneaked over him.

It was later, much later, that something woke him up.

But what?

He opened one eye. Then the other. He looked around.

Nothing.

Yes, something.

He raised one ear, then the other.

Every inch of him listened.

Nothing.

But still, still, something.

There was a slight whir, and a small squeak.
Lobo looked to the right, to the left.
Slowly his head came out from under the bush,
and then his shoulders.
Cautiously, the rest of him followed.

He stepped to the edge of the lawn.
He looked down the street. Nothing.
Then up the street. And there it was—whirring
and squeaking, and slowly coming right down the
sidewalk toward him.

Was it a friendly creature?

Was it a monster?

Its legs were strange. They were circles. Its body was like a big flat box, covered at one end.

Lobo cocked his head and looked hard.

The creature kept coming, coming.
Lobo couldn't hold himself back. He barked. He
barked louder.
Still it came closer.
Lobo ran forward three steps and barked.
He jumped back three steps and barked again.

Suddenly the round legs came to a ridge in the curb in front of Lobo, and there they stopped. Now there was another sound—a strange loud noise coming from inside the box.

Lobo stopped barking.
He walked cautiously up to the noise.

He stood on his two back legs so he could peer into the box.
He saw a tiny boy!

Much smaller than Peter, but still a boy. He had a red face and a wide-open mouth. He was crying. Lobo didn't blame him.

He was probably lonely.

But where was his family?

Lobo sat right under the carriage, so the little boy would know he was near, and he started to bark again. He barked the biggest bark he had inside him.

The carriage wheels jiggled against him, but Lobo sat still so the carriage couldn't move. He kept barking.

People started coming from all directions. Peter
and Mary Ann and their friends came running.
Mrs. McGee came dashing out.
Neighbors came from all sides, and best of all, the
baby's mother.

Quickly she picked him up, and little by little the
baby stopped crying.

"My goodness," the baby's mother said. "The carriage brakes must have come loose. This little dog found my baby."

"This little dog?" said one of the neighbors. "I thought I heard a huge ferocious dog barking."

"That was me," thought Lobo. "I'm the huge ferocious dog."
"Lobo's the huge ferocious dog," said Peter.
Lobo stood as tall as he could.
"Lobo's a hero!" said Mary Ann.

Lobo looked over his shoulder to the tip of his tail.
"I guess I really am little," he thought.

"Come on, Lobo," Peter said. "I'm going to give you a treat."

"Fine," Lobo said to himself as he followed Peter into the house.

"But I hope he doesn't get confused. I may be a little dog, but I like a big treat."